# CAT the CAT
# Who Is THAT?

by
## MO WILLEMS

Balzer + Bray

*An Imprint of* HarperCollins *Publishers*

# Cat the Cat, who is that?

# It's Mouse the Mouse!

Hi, Mouse the Mouse!

# Cat the Cat, who is that?

# It's Duck the Duck!

Hi, Duck the Duck!

# Cat the Cat, who is that?

# It's Fish the Fish!

Hi, Fish the Fish!

# Cat the Cat

# likes her friends!

# Cat the Cat, who is THAT?

EEP!

# It's a NEW friend!

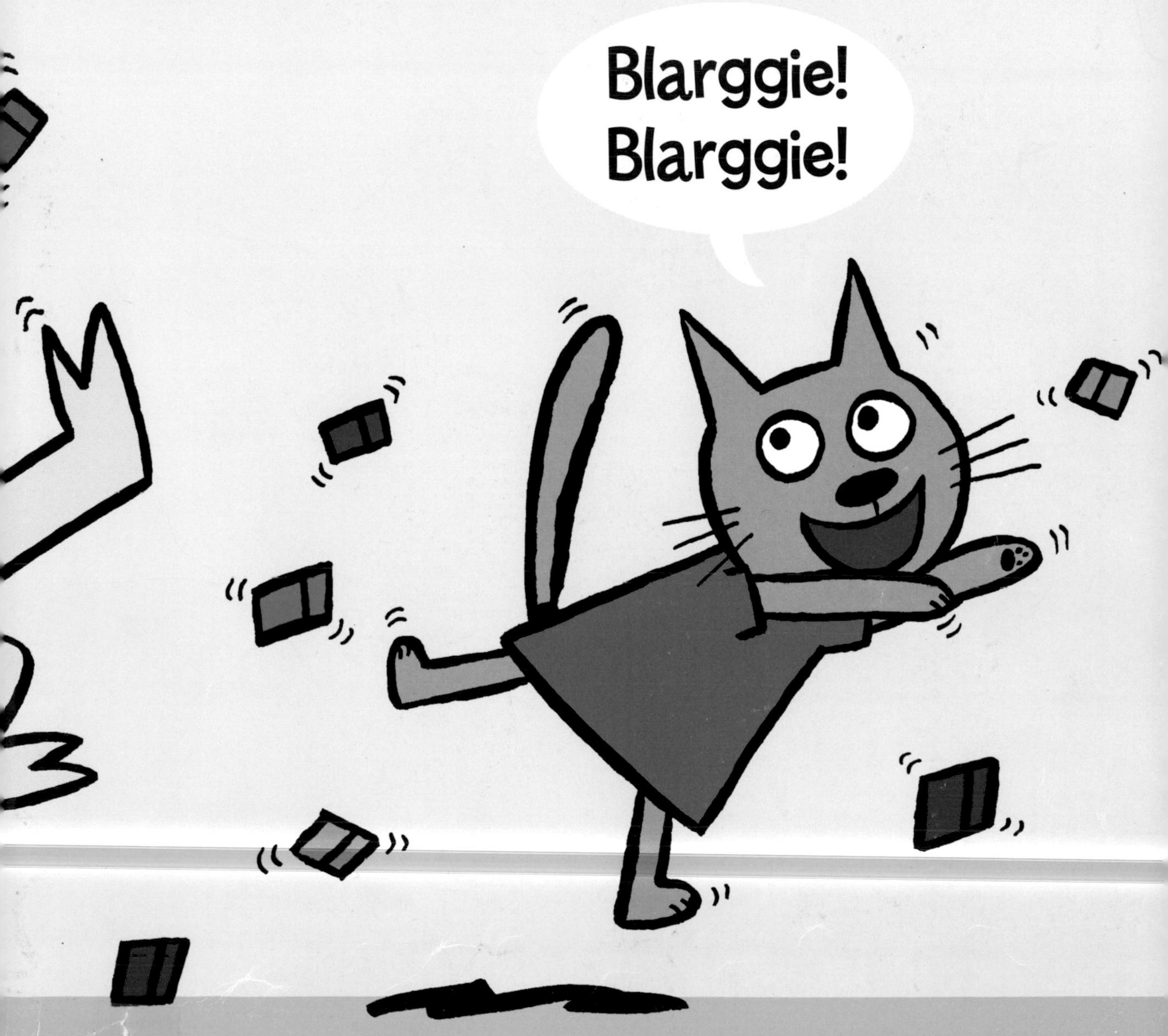

To my wife, Cher.
Blarggie! Blarggie!

Cat the Cat, Who Is THAT?
Copyright © 2010 by Mo Willems
Printed in the U.S.A.

Library of Congress Cataloging-in-Publication Data
Willems, Mo.
   Cat the cat, who is that? / Mo Willems. — 1st ed.
       p.    cm.
   Summary: An exuberant cat introduces readers to her friends.
   ISBN 978-0-06-172840-2 (trade bdg.) — ISBN 978-0-06-172841-9 (lib. bdg.)
   [1. Cats—Fiction.   2. Animals—Fiction.   3. Friendship—Fiction.]  I. Title.
PZ7.W65535Cat  2010                                  2008046187
[E]—dc22                                          CIP
                                                           AC

Typography by Martha Rago
10  11  12  13  14  LPR  10  9  8  7  6  5  4  3  2  1
❖
First Edition